Little One's Bedtime

For Alan David Moore
'Till China and Africa meet,
And the river jumps over the mountain
And the salmon sing in the street...' – SJM

To Darcy and Elliot – *RR*

SIMON AND SCHUSTER
First published in Great Britain in 2011 by Simon and Schuster UK Ltd
1st Floor, 222 Gray's Inn Road, London WC1X 8HB
A CBS Company

Text copyright © 2011 Suzi Moore
Illustrations copyright © 2011 Rosie Reeve
Design by Jane Buckley

The right of Suzi Moore and Rosie Reeve to be identified as
the author and illustrator of this work has been asserted by them
in accordance with the Copyright, Designs and Patents Act, 1988

A CIP catalogue record for this book is available from the British Library upon request

ISBN: 978-1-84738-671-7 (HB)
ISBN: 978-1-47115-809-4 (PB)

Printed in China
1 3 5 7 9 10 8 6 4 2

Little One's Bedtime

Suzi Moore and Rosie Reeve

SIMON AND SCHUSTER
London   New York   Sydney

It was late at night and time for bed.
The sky was dark when Somebody said,

"Come, Little One, Little One, come.
It's time to sleep, my Little One."

But Little One grumbled and Little One groaned.
"I'm not even tired," Little One moaned.

"I can't go to bed," Little One said. "Because . . .

I'm going to be a PIRATE instead!

Come along, Teddy, no time for a nap.
   There's gold to be found and I have the map.
Let's sail to the island, I know the way.
   We'll find all the treasure – anchors aweigh!"

It was late at night and time for bed.

    The clock was ticking when Somebody said,

"Come, Little Pirate, come in from the sea.

    Don't forget Teddy and come up with me."

But Little One stomped and jumped up and down.
"I'm still not tired," she said with a frown.

"I can't go to bed," Little One said. "Because . . .

I'm going to be a MONSTER instead!

Look! I'm a monster with a monstery nose.
I have monstery fingers and monstery toes.
Come along, Teddy, it's going to be great!
Monsters **always** stay up very late."

It was late at night and time for bed.
  The stars were twinkling when Somebody said,

"Come, Little Monster, Little One, come.
  Into the bathroom, Little One run."

So Little One ran and stood at the sink.
"I have an idea!" she said with a wink.

"I can't go to bed," Little One said. "Because . . .

I'm going to be a KNIGHT instead!

I'll ride to the castle with Teddy the Brave.

There's always a beautiful Princess to save.

Watch out for the dragon! I know what to do.

"Excuse me, fierce dragon, it's bedtime for you."

It was late at night and time for bed.

The moon was shining when Somebody said,

"Come, Little One, Little One, come.

It's getting late, my brave Little One."

But Little One jumped and sprang up to run.
Staying up late was always such fun.

"I can't go to bed," Little One said. "Because . . .

I'm going to be a DANCER instead!

I'll dance to the left, I'll dance to the right,
   I'm going to be a ballerina tonight.
Come along, Teddy, it's time for the show!
   I'm really quite famous or didn't you know?"

It was late at night and time for bed.

The stars were sparkling when Somebody said,
"Come, Little One, Little One, come.

Dance into your bedroom, my beautiful one."

So Little One danced and Little One pranced.
She'd stay up all night if she just got the chance.

"I can't go to bed," Little One said. "Because . . .

I'm going to be a WIZARD instead!

Come along, Teddy, there is magic to make.
Wizards don't sleep, they just stay awake!
I'll magic a rabbit right out of my hat.
I'll turn my big brother into a rat."

It was late at night and time for bed.

The owls were hooting when Somebody said,

"Come, Little One, Little One, come.
It's very late, my magical one.
Don't forget Teddy, climb up into bed.
No more adventures, it's bedtime instead."

Little One sighed and thought for a while.
"I am a bit tired," she said with a smile.

Under the covers Little One wriggled.
"I'll dream of adventure," Little One giggled.

Then Somebody kissed her and turned out the light.
"Sweet dreams, my Little One.

I love you. Goodnight!"